KU-754-510

ADELE GERAS
A Magic Birthday

Illustrated by Adriano Gon

SIMON & SCHUSTER
YOUNG BOOKS

Chapter One

"I like October best of all," said Maddy, sitting on the damp sand and letting the edges of frilly waves foam over her bare toes, "because it's my birthday month, and I'm having a party the day after tomorrow."

"I know" said her mother. "I've got it all under control. Just remind me of who's coming."

"Debbie and Jane and Sue and Polly and Diana. And Diana's got a long dress. She told me. Are you going to make a special cake?"

"Wait and see," said Mrs Roberts. "There'll be a surprise or two, that's all I'm saying. This," she went on, "is what I like best about the autumn. Being able to lie on the beach with my eyes closed."

Maddy giggled. "Most people take their clothes off to lie on the beach, not put on sweaters and duffle coats and old shoes."

"Silly them, then," said Mrs Roberts and closed her eyes.

Maddy said, "I like having you all to
myself, too, without any summer guests. I
like it when the sign on our house that says
'Belmont Private Hotel' gets switched off
for winter."

"But don't you miss them all?" Maddy's mother laughed.

"Mrs Fanshawe with her seaweed collection that made the bedroom smell for weeks, and Mr Bennett, who wanted a high chair for his dog?"

"No," said Maddy, "I don't really miss them, because I know we'll get more guests next year. And we've still got Mr Osborne."

Mrs Roberts said, "He's been staying so long he's like one of the family. He's a permanent fixture."

"What do you think he does, though," Maddy asked, "up in his room? He's got ever so many old books in there, and funny-looking bits and pieces. Are they to do with his work at the Bank?"

"I expect," said Mrs Roberts, "those are his hobbies. I've never really asked him. Now why don't you go and climb on the rocks, and come back in a few minutes?"

Maddy ran to the rocks, thinking about birthday cakes.

Last year, the cake had been in the shape of a train with three coaches: a lemon sponge coach, a chocolate coach and a coconut coach, all iced in different colours, with little faces made out of sweets peeping out of the windows.

Maddy never knew how her mother managed to paint in all the eyes and mouths and noses. But I was only six then, she thought. Mum probably did all the work when I was in bed. Maddy stayed up later now, but she hadn't seen any sign of a cake, and the party was so soon.

Suddenly, she smiled. It was silly to
worry about it. A party wasn't a party
without a cake, and there would be one, she
was quite sure. I'll have a look around in the
kitchen when we get home, she said to
herself, and concentrated on climbing the
rocks. The best beach of all was on the
other side.

Chapter Two

Maddy jumped on to the soft sand, and
started to walk to the edge of the water.
Then she stopped and ran back to crouch
behind a rock. Someone was standing with
his back to her: a man in a black cloak and a
tall, pointed purple hat with gold stars on
it, a wizard's hat.

Maddy watched from her hiding-place as a long line of silk scarves in rainbow colours appeared from the folds of his cloak, and floated on the sea breeze.

Then the scarves disappeared, and the man took his hat off, and pulled something out of it which was white, and flew higher and higher, up into the pale sky – a real bird, a dove.

Maddy stared at the back of the man's head. She felt she knew that head very well. It looked just like Mr Osborne's, and

yet . . . people who worked in banks didn't
do magic, did they? Should she run back
and tell her mother? What if the man were a
real wizard? Would he turn her into a frog?

I'll call his name from here, she decided, and then, if it's Mr Osborne, I'll go and talk to him, and if it's a real wizard, I'll climb back over the rocks as quickly as I can and fetch Mum.

"Mr Osborne," she shouted. "Mr Osborne!"

The man turned round. As soon as Maddy saw his pink face and gold-rimmed glasses, she recognized him.

"How clever you are!" she called,
running over the sand towards him.
"I never knew you could do magic!"

"Oh, dear," said Mr Osborne. "The cat
is, as they say, properly out of the bag."

"Is it a secret?" said Maddy. "I won't tell
anyone, honestly."

"Well, not many people know, do you
see? Some colleagues at the Bank, of
course . . . I did do a turn at the Christmas
party last year. Your dear mother knows,
of course, and well, you see, I am a mere
beginner, a novice. I like to practise here
sometimes. The sea, you know, and the
wind and sky do seem to help the magic."

"I think your tricks are smashing," said
Maddy. "I won't tell anyone if you don't
want me to."

Maddy wished she could tell all her friends about knowing a real magician. Nobody else had someone living in their house who could make a dove appear out of a hat.

"No, dear," said Mr Osborne. "It's not that I didn't want you to know, but your mother did ask me not to tell you so that it would be a surprise . . ." He frowned.

Maddy smiled. "I bet I can guess . . . she's asked you to do some magic tricks at my party, hasn't she? Oh, that's lovely!"

"Oh my goodness," said Mr Osborne, "now the beans are properly spilled, aren't they? I *am* sorry."

"I shan't say a word," Maddy promised. "It'll be wonderful having a real magician at the party."

"You think your friends would like that, do you?"

"Oh yes, Mr Osborne," said Maddy, throwing her arms around him and rumpling his cloak. "I've never had anything like that at a party before. It'll be . . . it'll be magic!"

"Magic?" said Mr Osborne. "I hope it will be. Yes, indeed."

"It will be," Maddy laughed. "Tremendously, hugely, enormously magical."

Chapter Three

The next day at school, Maddy's friends tried to guess what her cake would be like.

"I think," said Jane, "it'll be a clock."

"Mrs Roberts made a clock when we were in the infants," said Debbie. "You weren't here then, so you don't remember."

Polly said, "I had a cake once that was like a bed, with a lot of little mice in it."

"But yours came from a shop," said Sue.

"Doesn't matter," said Polly. "It was still a bed."

"There'll be a surprise," said Maddy, "but I'm not saying what it is."

"If you tell me," said Diana, "I'll give you half my crisps."

"Don't tell us, Maddy," said Debbie.
"It's not a surprise if everyone knows about
it before."

"Spoilsport," Diana pulled a face. "She
was going to tell me."

"I wasn't," said Maddy. "I never was.
You'll have to wait and see."

A surprise was all very well, Maddy
thought, but what about a cake? Perhaps
Mum is making it at this very moment.

Nothing at all had been baked by the time Maddy came home from school. Yesterday, after tea, she had looked in the larder for little paper bags full of decorations, and found none. The packet of icing sugar was nearly finished, and there were only two eggs in the fridge and those had been eaten at breakfast this morning.

She'd checked the cupboards today again, and everything was exactly the same as it had been yesterday.

Now she lay in bed listening very hard for sounds of cake-making from downstairs. She sniffed the air. No cooking smells anywhere. It was late. The clock downstairs had just struck nine o'clock, and she hadn't heard the usual noises: forks beating eggs, or cream being whipped or paper bags of sugar crunching and scrunching. There would be no cake. It was impossible. It was unbelievable, but it was true.

Maddy tried to remember whether her mother had said anything about a cake while they were on the beach. Hadn't she said it was going to be all right? Or under control? Then where was it?

Suddenly, Maddy knew. It was in the attic, where she slept during the summer, when visitors were using her bedroom. She jumped out of bed and listened on the landing, then she tiptoed up to the second floor, and upstairs again to the attic.

She opened the door as quietly as she could, and turned on the light.

There was a bed, a chest-of-drawers, a cupboard, a chair and a sink in the room, and that was all. Maddy smiled. The cupboard was the place, as sure as sure.

She looked inside and then looked again because she could hardly believe it – such a marvellous hiding-place and nothing in it: not a crumb, or a flour speck, or a grain of sugar.

Maddy ran back to her bed and covered her head with a blanket, trying hard not to cry. There was no doubt about it. There was no cake in the house and no time to make one now. Would having a magician make up for having no cake? Wondering about this, worrying about it, Maddy fell asleep.

Chapter Four

"Please pass the sausages," said Diana, in her long dress.

"May I have some more lemonade?" said Polly.

Debbie and Sue were whispering at the other side of the table and Maddy knew what they were whispering about. The table looked empty without a cake, even though pineapple and cheese cubes and sandwiches and nuts and raisins and crisps covered the tablecloth.

All the morning, Maddy had waited for a cake to be delivered to the house in the red van from the Pom-pom bakery, but here were the guests, this was the birthday tea and there was no cake. Still, everyone now knew what the surprise was, and they were being very polite and pretending that nothing was wrong.

"Are we really having a proper magician after tea?" Jane asked.

"Yes," said Maddy. "It's Mr Osborne."

"Mr Osborne?" said Polly. "But he works in a bank. Magicians don't work in banks."

Sue said, "I don't see why magicians can't work wherever they want to."

"Good magicians," said Diana, putting a whole handful of raisins into her mouth, "are on TV."

"I expect Mr Osborne might be on TV one day," said Debbie. "Have you seen any tricks, Maddy? Are they good?"

"I haven't seen very much," Maddy answered, "But once he took a real dove out of his hat and it flew right into the sky."

"That's nothing," said Polly. "All magicians pull things out of hats. Usually, it's rabbits."

"When you've finished your tea, girls," said Mrs Roberts, "go and sit in the lounge and I'll tell Mr Osborne he can begin."

Debbie and Jane and Sue and Polly and
Diana crumpled up their napkins and left
them among the crumbs on their plates as
they ran out of the room.

Maddy followed them to the lounge,
where they were sitting on the carpet,
laughing, waiting for the show to begin.

When Mr Osborne came into the room, everyone stopped talking. The only light came from the fire and a small lamp on the sideboard, and his gigantic shadow fell crookedly on the wall as he raised his arms in the black cloak, and the gold stars glittered on his pointed hat.

"Young ladies," he said gravely, "I am
going to mystify and delight you with my
magic. Watch carefully."

And they did.

They watched as playing cards appeared
from the folds of their dresses, they stared
as Mr Osborne drew scarves and
handkerchiefs from the cuffs of his shirt,
and brought out eggs from beneath the sofa
cushions, real eggs which he broke into a
bowl.

No one spoke, and even Diana's mouth
hung open in amazement as a silk scarf
flapped and rippled and turned into a white
dove which fluttered around
the room and landed on
Mr Osborne's shoulder.

"You, my beauty," said Mr Osborne, "must go back to your cage. Maddy, my dear, if you look just outside the door, you will find a bird-cage."

Maddy left the room, and Mr Osborne continued, "When she returns, my dear young ladies, I shall ask her to help me with my most amazing and baffling trick."

"Is this it, Mr Osborne?" said Maddy.

"Indeed it is," said Mr Osborne. "Now please bring it here and stay with me, if you would, to help me with my next trick."

"Me?"

"You are the birthday girl," said Mr Osborne, as he put the white dove into the cage and locked the door with a golden key. "Please check that this cage is locked."

"Yes," said Maddy. "I've looked at everything. It's locked."

"Now cover it with this cloth," said Mr Osborne, and handed Maddy a square of red velvet. When the cage was covered, Mr Osborne turned the lamp off.

"Now make a wish, Maddy," he said, "and everyone keep very still."

Maddy closed her eyes.

A cake. I wish for a cake, she thought. A beautiful cake in the shape of a castle, with a princess on the battlements, and turrets of white icing-sugar and blue icing-sugar water all around it. I wish, wish, wish for a cake.

She opened her eyes.

"There!" said Mr Osborne. "Turn on all the lights now. That's right. And Maddy, take off the magic cloth."

Maddy closed her eyes again and pulled at the red velvet. Suddenly everyone was clapping and shouting and saying, "Oh, Maddy, look! Look at that!"

Maddy looked, then looked again, and then reached into the cage and touched. There was her birthday cake.

"It's exactly, exactly what I wished for," she said. "Where did it come from? I can't believe it. Even the princess is there, look, on the battlements. How did you do it?"

"That," said Mr Osborne, "is a secret. But I do think it was a sensible thing to have wished for. I've never considered a birthday party complete without a birthday cake."

He opened the cage with the golden key
and took the cake out and presented it to
Maddy. She held it up so that everyone
could see it. Mr Osborne drew six plates
from under his arm and a sharp knife from
his breast pocket.

"Ms Maddy Roberts will now," he announced grandly, "come forward and cut the first slice!"